The Jenius

Dick King-Smith served in the Grenadier Guards during the Second World War, and afterwards spent twenty years as a farmer in Gloucestershire, the county of his birth. Many of his stories are inspired by his farming experiences. Later he taught at a village primary school. His first book, *The Fox Busters*, was published in 1978. Since then he has written a great number of children's books, including *The Sheep-Pig* (winner of the Guardian Award and filmed as *Babe*), *Harry's Mad*, *Noah's Brother*, *The Hodgeheg*, *Martin's Mice*, *Ace*, *The Cuckoo Child* and *Harriet's Hare* (winner of the Children's Book Award in 1995). At the British Book Awards in 1991 he was voted Children's Author of the Year. He has three children, a large number of grandchildren and several great-grandchildren, and lives in a seventeenth-century cottage only a crow's flight from the house where he was born.

Books by Dick King-Smith

ANIMAL STORIES
BACK-TO-FRONT BENJY
CLEVER DUCK
GEORGE SPEAKS
THE GHOST AT CODLIN CASTLE AND OTHER STORIES
THE HODGEHEG
THE INVISIBLE DOG
JULIUS CAESAR'S GOAT
THE JENIUS
THE MAGIC CARPET SLIPPERS
KING MAX THE LAST
A NARROW SQUEAK AND OTHER ANIMAL STORIES
PHILIBERT THE FIRST AND OTHER STORIES
MR POTTER'S PET
SMASHER
THE SWOOSE

Colour Young Puffins

BLESSU
DINOSAUR SCHOOL
DUMPLING
FAT LAWRENCE
POPPET
THE GREAT SLOTH RACE

Dick King-Smith
The Jenius

Illustrated by Ann Kronheimer

PUFFIN

PUFFIN BOOKS

Published by the Penguin Group
Penguin Books Ltd, 80 Strand, London WC2R 0RL, England
Penguin Group (USA), Inc., 375 Hudson Street, New York, New York 10014, USA
Penguin Books Australia Ltd, 250 Camberwell Road, Camberwell, Victoria 3124, Australia
Penguin Books Canada Ltd, 10 Alcorn Avenue, Toronto, Ontario, Canada M4V 3B2
Penguin Books India (P) Ltd, 11 Community Centre, Panchsheel Park, New Delhi – 110 017, India
Penguin Books (NZ) Ltd, Cnr Rosedale and Airborne Roads, Albany, Auckland, New Zealand
Penguin Books (South Africa) (Pty) Ltd, 24 Sturdee Avenue, Rosebank 2196, South Africa

Penguin Books Ltd, Registered Offices: 80 Strand, London WC2R 0RL, England

www.penguin.com

First published by Victor Gollancz Ltd 1988
Published in Puffin Books 1998
Published in this edition 2004
1

Text copyright © Fox Busters Ltd, 1988
Illustrations copyright © Ann Kronheimer, 2004
All rights reserved

The moral right of the author and illustrator has been asserted

Set in 17/22.25pt Perpetua

Made and printed in England by Clays Ltd, St Ives plc

British Library Cataloguing in Publication Data
A CIP catalogue record for this book is available from the British Library

ISBN 0–141–31286–6

Contents

1   Guinea Pigs Aren't Stupid   1

2   An Unexpected Arrival   6

3   Training   14

4   A Great Team   21

5   Die For Your Country!   31

6   A Nightmare   39

7   A Bit of a Bighead   46

8   Pets' Day   54

9   Eat Your Hat   65

1
Guinea Pigs Aren't Stupid

'If I was the Queen,' Judy said, 'I wouldn't have corgis.'

'What sort of dogs would you have, Judy?' said her teacher.

The class were talking about pets and which were their favourites.

'I wouldn't have dogs at all.'

'What would you keep then,' said

Judy's teacher, 'if you were the Queen?'

'Guinea pigs,' said Judy.

Everybody burst out laughing and Judy went very red.

'They're my favourite animals,' she said defiantly. 'If I was the Queen I'd keep lots of them.'

'In hutches, you mean?'

'No. In Buckingham Palace.'

'But Judy,' said her teacher, 'wouldn't it look rather odd if someone very important came to call, like, say, the President of the United States of America, and the Queen, I mean you, said "Do take a seat, Mr President", and there was

a guinea pig lying in the
armchair?'

'And there'd be
messes all over the
carpet,' someone said.
'And
the President
would step in them,' said
someone else.

Everybody giggled.

'My guinea pigs would be house-
trained,' muttered Judy, close to
tears.

'Palace-trained, you
mean,' said a voice, and
now there was so
much sniggering that
the teacher said

'That's enough, children.'

She put her hand on Judy's shoulder and said: 'It's a nice idea, but even if you were the Queen you wouldn't be able to train a guinea pig like you can train a dog. Only certain animals are intelligent enough to be taught things by humans, and I'm afraid guinea pigs are not among them. They're dear little creatures, Judy, but they haven't got a lot of brains.'

2
An Unexpected Arrival

'You *have* got a lot of brains,' said Judy.

As always, she had run down to the shed at the bottom of the garden the moment she arrived home from school, to see her own two guinea pigs. One was a reddish rough-haired boar called Joe and the other was a smooth-coated white sow by the name of Molly. Judy had had

them ever since her sixth birthday, nearly
two years ago now, and they were very
dear to her. Her only regret was that,
surprisingly, they had never had babies.

'You *have* got brains,' she said, 'I'm
sure of it. It's just that no one's ever
taught you to use them. Now, if I'd had
you when you were tiny, I bet I could
have taught you lots of things. If only
you'd had children of your own. I'd have
chosen one of them and kept it and really
trained it, from a very early age. I bet I

could have done.'

As usual, the guinea pigs responded to the sound of her voice by beginning a little conversation of their own. First Joe made a grumbling sort of chatter (which meant 'Molly, you're as lovely now as the day I first set eyes on you'), and then Molly gave a short shy squeak (which meant 'Oh Joe, you say the nicest things!').

Then they both squealed long and loudly at Judy. She knew what that noise meant. They were telling her to cut the cackle and dish up the grub.

'Greedy old things,' she said, and she picked up the white one, Molly.

'Molly!' said Judy. 'You look awfully fat. Whatever's the matter with you?'

Molly didn't reply. Joe grunted in a self-satisfied sort of way.

'I'll have to put you on a diet,' said Judy firmly, 'starting tomorrow.'

But next morning, when she went to feed the guinea pigs, the white one, she found, looked quite different.

'Molly!' said Judy. 'You look awfully thin. Whatever's the matter with you?'

This time they both answered,

Molly with a series of small happy squeaks and Joe with a low proud grumble, as they moved aside to show what had happened. There between them was a single, very large, baby guinea pig, the child of their old age. It was partly white and smooth like its mother and partly red and rough like its father.

To Judy's delight it stumbled forwards on feet that seemed three sizes too big, until it bumped the wire of the hutch-front with its huge head. Its eyes were very bright and seemed to shine with intelligence. Then it spoke a single word in guinea pig language. Anyone could have told it meant 'Hullo!'

'Oh!' said Judy. 'Aren't you beautiful!'

'He gets it from his mother,' chattered

Joe in the background.

'And aren't you brainy!'

'He takes after his dad,' squeaked Molly.

Judy stared into the baby's eyes.

'You,' she said, 'are going to be the best-trained, most brilliant guinea pig in the whole world. And you're going to start lessons right away. Now then. Sit!'

Of course, when you're only a few hours old, standing can be tiring, but was that the reason why Joe and Molly's son immediately sat down?

3
Training

That night, before she went to bed, Judy
wrote the great news in her diary. She
was very faithful about putting
something in it every day, even if
sometimes it was only a bit about the
weather. But that Joe and Molly should
have had a baby – that was great news
and deserved a lot of space.

JUDY'S DIARY. PRIVIT.

JUNE 10th: Great surprise! Molly had a baby! Found him first thing this morning and I am going to train him. Alreddy he sits when he is told. He is briliant. He is mostly white like Molly but he has a sort

of main like a horse running all
down his back and that is reddish
like Joe.

I asked Dad what you call
someone who is really briliant and
he said 'A jenius. Why?' and I said
'because that is what I'm going to
call my new baby guinea pig' and
he laughed but I said 'You just
wait. One day the World will know
June 10th is the birthday of
Jenius.'

June 10th was in fact a very good time
for Jenius to have been born, because it
meant that he was around six weeks old
by the time the long summer holidays
began. Now his trainer would be able to

concentrate on him without the
interruption of school.

During those six weeks Jenius had
grown amazingly. All baby guinea pigs
do, of course, but he had benefited
particularly, first from being an only
child and so getting all his mother's milk,
and secondly from Judy's spoiling.

Ordinary guinea pigs, for example,
might get the occasional piece of stale

bread. Jenius got regular digestive biscuits.

So that Judy's diary, which had contained daily reports of the progress of the wonder child, read . . .

JULY 22nd: Begining of Summer Hollidays. Today I took Jenius away from his parents and put him in the spare hutch, he is reddy to start his training, he is alreddy half as big as Joe, he is alreddy very good at sitting when he is told because that is what I have consentrated on but now I am going to teach him 'Come' and 'Stay' and 'Down'. Joe and Molly don't seem to miss him.

Joe and Molly were actually quite glad to see the back of Jenius.

Molly was thankful not to be nagged for the milk she no longer had, and Joe, though at first proud of the obvious cleverness of his son, was growing tired of being patronized.

'Thinks he knows it all,' he grumbled to Molly, 'with his "No, Dad, you've got that wrong" or "No, Dad, you don't understand". I said to him: "When you've

been around as long as I have, my boy, then maybe you'll know a thing or two".'

'Quite right, dear,' murmured Molly. 'What did he say then?'

'He said: "When I've been around as long as you have I'll know hundreds of things". Cheeky young devil!'

'Ah well,' sighed Molly. 'He's only young, Joe dear. We're all of us only young once.'

'Molly,' said Joe, 'you're as lovely now as the day I first set eyes on you.'

'Oh Joe,' said Molly, 'you say the nicest things!'

4
A Great Team

'Mum! Mum!' cried Judy, bursting in
from the garden with Jenius in her arms.
'Guess what!'

'Not now, Judy,' said her mother. 'I
haven't got time for guessing games this
morning what with the washing and the
ironing, and I've got a lot of cooking to
do, never mind the housework. Off you

run and play, out of my way, please.'

'But Mum, Jenius comes when he's told!'

'Very clever, dear. Now you go when you're told, there's a good girl.'

'She just didn't listen to what I was saying,' said Judy as she sat on the lawn with Jenius on her lap.

Jenius replied with a small sympathetic

whistle which meant, Judy felt sure,
'Grown-ups are hopeless, aren't they? I
expect it'll be just the same when you
tell your dad.'

And it was.

'Comes when you call him, does he?'
said her father from behind his evening
paper.

'Yes, Dad! Honest! Don't you want to see?'

'Not now, pet, I've had a long day. You go and teach your precious genius something else.'

'What like?'

'Oh, reading, writing, some sums. Start with the two-times table – guinea pigs are good at multiplying. Buzz off now, there's a good girl.'

JULY 23rd: I think Mum and Dad grew up in Vicktorian days, they think that childeren should be seen and not herd. I am not going to bother to tell them anything about Jenius any more but only write about him in this dairy so

that the World will know how
clever he is when I am DED Dead
and Gone.

In the darkness of the garden shed Jenius
squeaked from the spare hutch: 'Mum!
Dad! Guess what!'

'Not now, dear,' said Molly.

'But guess what I learned today!'

'Hundreds of things, I imagine,' said Joe sourly.

'No, only one. I learned to come when called.'

'Well, now learn to shut up,' said Joe. 'It's late.'

'Your father's right, dear,' said Molly. 'Go to sleep now, there's a good boy.'

Throughout those fine sunny summer holidays the flowering of Jenius came into full bloom.

Judy was the ideal trainer, patient and hard-working, and her new pet was the perfect pupil. He enjoyed his lessons, he learned quickly, and what he had learned he seldom forgot. They made a great team.

AUGUST 15th: Here is a list of the things I have trained Jenius to do:

1. COME
2. SIT
3. STAY
4. DOWN
5. WALK ON A LEED
(I do not make him walk to heal because I might tred on him so he walks a little bit in front of me.)

Before the end of the Hollidays I am going to teach him three speshial tricks

(A) 'Speak'. That is to make a noise when he is told (I suppose I should call this 'SQUEAK').

(B) 'Trust'. That is balancing a bit of biskit on his nose.

(C) 'Die For Your Country'. He has to lie quite still with his eyes shut pretending to be Dead. If I can teach him all these things before the begining of Term I will take him to school and show them all just what a <u>Jenius</u> can do.

Every day trainer and trainee worked at their lessons. And every night Jenius kept his aged parents awake long after their

proper bedtime, telling
them all the clever
things he had learned
to do. He had
become, it must be
said, a bit of a bighead.

Molly, who was
rather vague by
nature, did not
listen very
carefully to her
son's boasting,
and only yawned

and said, 'Very
nice, dear,' now
and then, but
Joe became
irritable.

'You must be the most brilliant guinea pig there has ever been,' he would say sourly, but this did not improve matters, for Jenius always replied: 'I am, Dad, I am,' in a voice so smug that it made Joe's teeth chatter with rage.

'Cocky young blighter,' he would mutter to Molly. 'One of these fine days he's going to be too clever for his own good.'

And Joe was right. One of those fine days came quite soon.

5

Die For Your Country!

Jenius had woken early. He looked out of
the shed door (which Judy always left
open on warm nights) and saw a number
of attractive things outside in the garden.
There were lettuces and cabbages and
the feathery tops of carrots and the shiny
dark leaves of beetroot — all very
appealing to a growing lad. Why wait to

be fed, he thought. I'll feed myself.

'Mum!' he called. 'I'm going for a walk.'

Molly came to the front of her hutch and looked across the shed.

'Don't be silly, dear,' she said. 'You can't.'

Joe joined her.

'In case you hadn't noticed,' he said sarcastically, 'there's a door on the front of your hutch.'

'Dad,' said Jenius in a patient tone of voice, 'doors are meant to be opened.'

'I know that, boy. By humans. From outside. Not by us from inside. If you can open the door of that hutch from inside, I'll eat my hayrack.'

Each hutch had an outward-opening wire door, kept shut by a two-inch turn button, a simple device capable of keeping prisoner every guinea pig that had ever lived. Except the Jenius.

Sitting up on his bottom as he had
learned, he reached a forepaw through
the wire mesh and turned the button
vertically. The door swung open, and
down he hopped.

He paused at the entrance to the shed.

'Dad,' he called, 'don't forget to eat
your hayrack,' and off he trotted.

What happened next was recorded by a
short dramatic entry in the diary.

AUGUST 26th: Jenius got out and was nearly killed! I am keeping the door of the shed shut in case he esscapes again.

Jenius was sitting happily in the sunlit vegetable garden, nibbling a tender young lettuce plant and thinking what a

clever chap he was, when he heard his
name called. He looked up and saw Judy
leaning out of her bedroom window.

'Whatever are you doing out there?'
she said, and since Jenius made no reply,
she issued two commands.

'Sit!' she said, and 'Stay!'

Jenius obediently sat down, quite content to remain where he was, in easy reach of such nice food.

Judy was just turning away from her window when to her horror she saw the big tabby tom cat from next door drop down from the dividing wall. Slowly, stealthily, he began to stalk the lettuce-eater.

Judy thought frantically. If she left Jenius dutifully sitting and staying, he was a goner. If she called 'Come!' the cat would surely overtake him before she could get downstairs.

There was only one thing to be done, only one order she could give that might perhaps puzzle the hunter for long enough for her to rush to the rescue.

'Jenius!' she yelled in the fiercest, most commanding voice she could manage. 'Die For Your Country!'

6
A Nightmare

Jenius, accustomed as he now was to receiving odd orders at odd times, instantly collapsed flat on his back. He stopped chewing his mouthful of lettuce, he closed his eyes, and even the rise and fall of his ribs seemed to have stopped, so lightly did he breathe. He lay, slack and still, looking every inch as he was meant

to look. Dead.

'Dead!' said a voice in his ear suddenly.

Jenius's blood ran cold at the sound of this harsh, cruel voice, at the smell of hot, rank breath, at the tickle of long whiskers as something sniffed him all over.

'Pity,' said the cat. 'Could have had a bit of sport if you'd been alive. Ah well, a dead tail-less rat is better than no rat at all,' and with that he began to lick at his victim's head.

Try as he would, Jenius could not keep his upper eye shut. Under the rasp of the cat's tongue the eyelid was pulled back, and he saw, only inches away, a nightmare face. A merciless face it was, with glowing yellow eyes and a wide mouth

filled with sharp white teeth. Despite
himself, Jenius gave a little shudder.

'Aha!' hissed the cat. 'Not dead after
all!' and he opened that wide mouth. But
before he could close it again, a clod of
earth hit him on the ear and a furious
voice yelled, 'Scat!' as Judy came
galloping to the rescue. She knelt among
the lettuce plants beside the motionless

figure of the Jenius.

'It's all right!' she cried. 'He's gone. You can get up now.'

As always she used the system of praise-and-reward by which she had trained him.

'*What* a good boy!' she said, and from the pocket of her dungarees she took one of his favourite digestive biscuits and broke off a bit.

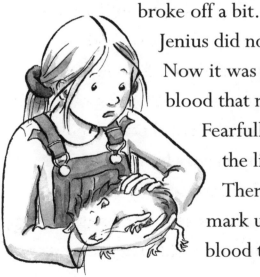

Jenius did not move. Now it was Judy's blood that ran cold. Fearfully she lifted the limp body. There was no mark upon it, no blood to be seen.

Could he have died of shock?

'Jenius!' cried Judy frantically in his
ear. 'Speak to me. Speak!'

Even though he had fainted with fear at
the sheer horror of the experience, the

sound of a familiar command was enough to bring him to his senses.

Feebly, through that unchewed mouthful of lettuce, the Jenius obediently uttered a single strangled squeak.

It was a much-reduced Jenius that Judy replaced in his hutch, and when Molly asked: 'Had a nice walk, dear?' he did not answer.

'What's the matter, son?' said Joe. 'Cat got your tongue?'

7
A Bit of a Bighead

AUGUST 26th: Jenius escaped a
horribel Death!

Jenius had no intention of escaping again.
He had had the fright of his life and, for a
little while, his parents were spared their
son's bragging and they could enjoy some
early nights.

But before long he forgot, and his natural cockiness returned, particularly when he at last mastered the most difficult trick of the exercises that Judy set him. This was the ending to the trick called 'Trust'.

Not only had he to balance a piece of  biscuit on the end of his nose, but then, when Judy said 'Paid for!', he had to toss up the food with a jerk of his head and catch it in his mouth. Jenius never tired of telling his mother and father how easy this trick was.

'Mind you,' he said, 'I'm the only guinea pig in the world who can do it, I'm sure of that.'

'Very nice, dear,' said Molly absently.

'Pride,' muttered Joe darkly, 'comes before a fall.'

SEPTEMBER 3rd: Jenius has quite recovered. Tomorrow is the last day of the Hollidays and I am going to give him a Test. I am going ~~the~~ to make him do all the things he has been taut and he has got to do them correcktly and I shall give him marks for his performants in each one.

SEPTEMBER 4th: Jenius lived up to his name! He performed perfictly and got Full Marks and I am going to ask my teacher if I can take him to school and show them how briliant he is and how briliantly I have trained him. I'm the only person in the World who could have done it, I'm sure of that.

Jenius, it must be said, was not the only one who had become a bit of a bighead, and by the end of the first day back at school everyone in the class was fed up with hearing how clever both he and Judy were. Before long Judy's teacher too had had enough.

'Judy,' she said. 'You don't really expect
us to believe all this, do you?'

'Yes,' said Judy. 'It's true.'

'Well, I'll tell you what. You bring this
amazing animal of yours into school and

then you can show us all these tricks that
you say he can do.'

At once everyone wanted to get in on
the act and bring their pet
to school.

'Oh, can I bring my
rabbit?'

'. . . my gerbil?'

'. . . my hamster?'

'. . . my budgie?'

Until the teacher said: 'All right. We'll
have a Pets' Day. You can each bring a pet
in to school, provided
you bring it in a cage
or a box — we don't
want anything
too big, mind,
no Shetland

Ponies or Great
Danes. Who
knows, Judy,
someone else
may have a clever
animal too.'

Judy laughed. 'Not as clever as Jenius,'
she said scornfully. 'Not possibly. You just
wait and see.'

8
Pets' Day

Like most people who keep diaries, Judy
wrote in hers each evening. But as soon
as she woke on the morning that had
been chosen for Pets' Day, she opened it.

SEPTEMBER 11th: Today it is Pets'
Day at school! Jenius will
tryumph! * Watch this space! *

At breakfast time she could not contain
herself. Till now she had said nothing to
her parents — as she had sworn on July
23rd — of the progress of the Jenius, but
she just knew she would not be able to
resist describing the success that was to
come before another hour had passed.

'What d'you think is happening today?'
she said.

'You're going to be late for school,' said
her mother, 'if you don't hurry up. And
clean your shoes before you go. And take
your anorak – it looks like rain.'

'I'm taking Jenius to school,' said Judy.

'Very nice, dear,' said her mother.
'Now, do you want an apple or a banana
in your lunch box?'

'Apple,' said Judy. 'Dad, did you hear
what I said?'

'I did,' said her father from behind his
morning paper. 'Will he have to start in
the Infants or is he clever enough to go
straight into your class?'

'Oh Dad!' cried Judy. 'Honestly, I
really have trained him,' and she rattled
off a list of the things that Jenius could
do.

'Judy,' said her father. 'You don't really
expect us to believe all this, do you?'

'Yes,' said Judy. 'It's true.'

Her father folded his newspaper.

'Now look here,' he said. 'Playing pretend games with your precious pet is one thing. But you mustn't confuse fantasy with truth.'

There was hardly room to move in Judy's classroom that morning.

Everywhere there were hutches and cages and baskets and boxes containing pets. Only the Jenius was free, sitting perfectly still in front of Judy.

Judy's teacher saw what seemed to her a rather odd-looking whitish guinea pig, with a crest of reddish hair sticking up along its back, and said: 'Is this the genius we've heard such a lot about?'

'Yes,' said Judy proudly. 'Shall I show you what he can do?'

'All right,' said her teacher. 'Put him on that big table in the middle of the room where everyone can see him.'

Ranged around the edges of the big table were several pet-containers: a couple of hamster-cages, a glass jar that held stick insects and a square basket that had one open side barred with metal rods.

Fate decreed that Judy should put the Jenius down quite near to this basket and facing it, and though no one else could see what was in it, he could. He looked through the bars and saw a face, a merciless face, with glowing yellow eyes and a wide mouth filled with sharp white teeth.

In fact the occupant of the basket was

only a half-grown kitten, but the sight of it turned Jenius's legs to jelly and scrambled his brains. He was so frightened that he promptly Died For His Country, and there he lay, quite still and barely breathing. He could hear Judy's

voice

saying, 'Come!'

and then, more

loudly, 'Jenius! Come!!' Then he heard a
rising tide of noise which was the whole
class first sniggering, then giggling, and
finally laughing their heads off at clever
Judy and her clever guinea pig, about

which she had boasted so loud and long.
But he could not move a muscle.

'The great animal trainer!' someone
said, and they laughed even more.

'Perhaps that will teach you a lesson,
Judy,' said the teacher at last. 'He doesn't

seem to be quite the genius you told us he was. You mustn't confuse fantasy with truth.'

9
Eat Your Hat

'How did you get on, dear, your first day at school?' said Molly that evening.

'Need you ask?' growled Joe. 'You were top of the class, weren't you, son? Got full marks for everything? Performed perfectly, eh?'

'No,' said the Jenius in a small choked voice. 'I didn't do anything.'

'Well well well,' said Joe. 'The only guinea pig in the world who can do all those tricks and he didn't do anything. I quite expected you to tell us you did something fantastic . . . Hopping like a rabbit perhaps. Or flying like a bird, I shouldn't be surprised.'

Judy came in at that moment with a bunch of dandelions, to hear Joe and Molly making an awful racket. She thought they were yelling for food as usual but actually they were in fits of laughter.

'Flying! Oh Joe, you are a scream!'
squealed Molly, and Joe, snorting with
mirth, chuckled, 'Pride comes before a
crash-landing!'

A few minutes later Judy's father, home
from work, put his head in at the door of
the shed.

'Well?' he said. 'And did our genius
perform all his amazing tricks?'

'No,' said Judy. 'He wouldn't do
anything.'

'Perhaps that will teach you a lesson,
Judy,' said her father.

Judy took a deep breath.

'Perhaps it has, Dad,' she said. 'But I
wouldn't like you to think I was a liar.'

'It's difficult for me not to think that,'
said her father, 'when you tell me such

fantastic things. For instance, that your
guinea pig can balance something on his
nose and then throw it up and catch it. If

he can do that,
I'll eat my hat, I
promise you.'

'Watch,' said
Judy. She took a
digestive out of
her pocket and
broke a piece off. She opened the door of
Jenius's hutch.

'Come!' she said, and he came.

'Sit!' she said, and he sat.

Carefully she placed the fragment of
biscuit on top of
Jenius's snout.

'Trust!' she said,
and he remained
sitting bolt upright
and stock-still for

perhaps ten
seconds, till Judy
cried, 'Paid for!'

Up in the air
sailed the bit of
digestive and down
it came again,
straight into the
open mouth of the Jenius.

'*What* a good boy!' said Judy. 'Now you
can eat it up.'

She turned
to her father,
who was
bending down,
hands on knees,
watching in
open-mouthed

amazement, hat in hand. She took it from
him.

'And you,' she said, 'can eat that.'